Tabby Cat chases a mouse.

The mouse runs away.

Tabby Cat chases a butterfly.

The butterfly flies away.

Tabby Cat chases a frog.

The frog hops away.

Tabby Cat chases a flower.

Good catch, Tabby Cat!

Tabby Cat swats a potato.

BUMP! Away goes the potato.

Tabby Cat swats a carrot.

THUMP! Away goes the carrot.

Tabby Cat swats a tomato.

SPLAT! Away goes the tomato.

Oh, oh! Here comes Mommy!

SCAT! Away goes Tabby Cat.

Tabby Cat washes her paw.

Tabby Cat washes her ear.

Tabby Cat washes her nose.

Tabby Cat washes her leg.

Tabby Cat washes her back.

Tabby Cat washes her tail.

Now Tabby Cat is all clean.

So Tabby Cat washes Sammy.

Tabby Cat eats her food.

But she is still hungry.

Tabby Cat hunts near a tree.

Tabby Cat hunts near a plant.

Tabby Cat hunts near a rock.

Tabby Cat hunts near a fence.

Tabby Cat hunts near Sammy.

Mmmm! Lots of good food here.